Shadow Attack on Old Edo

Andrew J. Cooper & Sootjarit Kirinhakone

Shadow Attack on Old Edo
By Andrew J. Cooper
Sootjarit Kirinhakone

For Our Parents

Thanks to everyone who had a part, supported and
believed in this project.

Special shout out to our friends on Facebook.

Contents

Introduction

“Shadow Attack on Old Edo” is what happens when two kids (we were somewhere between 10 – 12 years old) build a community online to be good guys and build a coalition of friends to protect kids interacting on PlayStation with avatars. We started roleplaying battles and sharpening our battle/writing skills. I even created a private roleplaying community that was safe on a personal website my parents helped me setup. I lost track of the site's activities, but the community kept growing without our knowledge. Fast forward, while online, a familiar name popped up in a gaming community and it was as if the conversations had never ended. The roleplaying battles moved to Facebook in a new community and was back on track. "Shadow Attack on Old Edo" is an expanded version of one of those battles.

Point of View Roleplay is a unique kind of roleplay. It features two or more people writing a story. However, each piece is written from their character's perspective. This story is written by me (Andrew Cooper) and a good friend of mine (Sootjarit Kirinhakone or Sujit for short). The characters featured in this story are Gida and the Shadow Reapers. Some parts may be repetitive, that is because we are establishing our character's perspective on the previous paragraphs. So, if an attack is launched in one paragraph, you may see it get mentioned again in another, due to one of the characters just now seeing it. All characters in this story belong to me, Alexander Frost, and Sujit. Rights to Starblades and Shadow Reapers belong to Alexander Frost. He has given me and Sujit approval to use his content in this story. Enjoy!

Chapter One

During dusk and towards night, the Shadow Reapers took over Old North Edo Pass. Old North Edo Pass is a fort that stood in the way of the road to Old Edo city. The military troops stationed there were not well suited to fight Shadow Reapers and had to evacuate the outpost and retreat to the main city. The guards never expected their least attacked border tower to be targeted, considering there were the natural barriers of the many mountains making it hard to navigate through and even reach the border. This was of no difficulty to the Shadows. These were beings who found ways around physical obstacles.

Shadow Reapers have power to control the shadows, to slip through space, and to fight like no other. They use soul-based attacks as they are masters of the soul. Their reputation of being strong adversaries is proved by their fighting with Timelords without the use of time to counter their time manipulation. Their clan was near extinct with their Limbo Realm no longer truly existing until Shadao Kezanami. The Limbo world, the Shadow Lands, the Land of Lost Souls; they have returned and so have the Shadow Reapers and their creatures.

The fortress was taken over by the Shadow Reapers swiftly within an hour, before night. Military troops of the New Genzhere Alliance are in defensive positions to defend the city. Both within and near the city, as well as up on the mountains between the city and the fortress.

The New Genzhere Alliance (NGA) is an organization comprised of multiple guilds for the sake of justice. Like any other organization made for the sake of good, where heroes can be born, they carry out the duties to fulfill justice where it is needed. They secure peace, with limited order and political force. With these virtues of peace, justice, and serenity they believe a good world can be conserved, and bad evil worlds can be liberated from their source. They are named "New" Genzhere rather than simply Genzhere because they are driven by their commitment to staying true to the very reason they were created. The many mistakes the previous ancestral organizations of similar structure made, will always be noted so that New Genzhere does not fall like the others. Like a brand-new car, while a car can last the car will continue to maintain its appearance and performance as "new". New Genzhere is in a league with multiple guilds, more notably the Guardians of Faith and the Sapphire Ravens. While NGA centers around its guilds, their leaders and advisors who make up the high council of NGA, consist of not only guild members, but independent enforcers that possess a skill over fighting ability or tactics. This deems them respect and leadership over others. To make peace and work smoothly over the multiverse, their alliance also welcomes leaders of other organizations and realms such as Heaven and gods/goddesses. For the sake of warfare with minor forces like armies rather than strong individual powered beings, New Genzhere Alliance as a military faction, has military captains participating in the high council.

An NGA trooper is on his knee looking closely into the scope of his sniper, firing his Holy Bullets into the Shadow Reapers making their way up the road on the mountain. The other troopers up close are rapidly firing their blasters. The Shadow Reapers were letting the physical attacks phase through them and evading shots when necessary, flying around like spirits. They fired back bolts of shadows appearing three-dimensional, burning the very souls of the NGA soldiers from their magic. From a distance as seen when in the villages of Old Edo District, small flashes of light could be seen up near the mountain regions. To the citizens, they looked like comets and shooting stars of yellow and greyish black. A pretty sight to see, but a tragic one. A bit of smoke could be seen on and behind the mountains.

As the many small battles in the mountain regions raged on in a stalemate situation, a good portion of the Shadow Reapers which included more of their elites, guarded their new fortress they've taken over. Standard Shadow Reapers roamed around likes spirits, circling the fortress and watching below the bridges. Up on the bridges and walls were stronger Shadow Reapers.

"Oh wow, all my time on this planet and I've never seen this place." A man says while walking through the cold mountainous area as if it were summer.

This man is African American, 6'2, and weighed 195 pounds. He is wearing a red sleeveless shirt which showed off his toned and muscular arms. He also had on black sweatpants with red trim. He had short black hair and white/black running shoes on.

As he continued walking, he couldn't help but notice the rustic design to the buildings as he drew closer to the city. However, he was snapped out of his thoughts due to his senses. He could hear screaming, wailing, and what sounded like guns firing. For a town this far off the map, it seems they were caught up in technology at least. The man could sense some strange energy coming from deep in the mountains and could feel the energy of above average people.

"There must be a battle going on, maybe I should help out... it's what dad would do." The man thinks to himself as he walks around a bend and happens to see the NGA trooper on his knee, firing an advanced sniper into the distance.

As to not startle the trooper, the man raised his hands above his head to show him he was friendly.

"Excuse me sir, what's going on here and do you need help?" The man asked.

The soldier with the sniper was startled by seeing someone appear within his proximity so suddenly amidst a battle. He calmed down when he realized the 6'2 male was no Shadow Reaper and showed signs of friendliness. The sniper quickly drops a device that created a quarter-sphere, dark blue energy barrier that faced the enemy direction so that they were protected. The barrier seemed to be powered by electricity that was highly intensified to create physical energy barriers.

"Oh good. One of you guys are here." The soldier said, assuming the man was part of the guild.

Usually those who would offer help to the soldiers were from New Genzhere. Having experience with working with guild members who are either superhuman in some form or supernatural, the sniper could tell the man possessed powers that were not among the average human population.

"Yes, we could really use some help. Maybe more help than you alone can provide, but don't worry. We sent a distress signal to our HQ earlier and they'll get more of you to help. However, since you're the first one here, there are more opportunities at stake. Right now, I think we can hold them off at this defensive position. It'll take a while if we were to just push through head on, because they will do the same and bring in more forces. Not all those Shadows have reached this area yet." He paused to

think, even pausing his hand gestures before continuing, though going straight to the point now.

"Look, this all started with them attacking our fort up north that acted as a border pass and defense. They took it over and are using that to facilitate their continuous attacks. If we don't get our fort back, this will either be an endless battle on the mountains, or they'll break through and eventually reach the city. Since you sneaked up on me easily, I'm sure you can sneak through their lines to infiltrate and attack them right at their heart directly... and immediately take them out!" The soldier emphasized as his eyes widen.

The barrier starts to melt from multiple Shadow Bolts fired at them from the Shadow Reapers. The sniper gets back down and resumes fire. This time he loaded different ammo into his magazine that provided better damage.

The man listened to the sniper intently. He then looked in the direction of the fort when it was referenced.

"Got it, my name is Gida and I'll do my best to reclaim that fort." Gida said to the sniper.

Gida is a Mutant. Mutants are humans whose cells and DNA are modified/altered to enhance them in combat and other areas of life. To create a Mutant, one must derive cells from an animal or being and splice them together with that of a human. This will give the newborn traits of those animals or beings and sometimes give it the appearance of the dominant trait. Gida's main appearance is that of a human and he contains dragon and wolf-like features.

Gida is a Gifted Mutant. A Gifted Mutant is a being whose cells and DNA have been enhanced to balance every aspect of their life. So not only is he gifted in the art of battle but also at socializing, romance, business, etc. Gida is a Mutant who lives to fight for those who can't fight to protect themselves. This often means he travels to many different planets. He loves the thrill of battle but also fears its consequences at times. He is a very patient and strategic fighter who will draw out battles just to find the right opening to beat his opponent. He doesn't enjoy killing but if he must then he won't hesitate to do so. Other than that, Gida is a kind and gentle fellow who fights to maintain peace throughout the universe. He is the son of a warrior named Emel. This warrior is a powerful Mutant who has strangely gone missing. Gida now travels the universe in search of his father.

Unable to fly, Gida crouched and maneuvered his way throughout the mountain. He used rocks, snow mounds, and edges as cover as he made his way out of the mountain. Once out of the battleground, Gida made his way towards Old North Edo Pass.

It was quite a trek but eventually Gida made it there.

Chapter Two

Once inside, Gida took in the sights of the fort. He soon snapped out of it though as he remembered why he is here. He heard strange sounds coming from three different parts of the fort. Gida concluded that there are multiple Shadows in each sector. He ran into the middle of the intersection and pointed his right hand towards the right path, and his left hand down the middle path. He began firing white energy blasts the size of his hands from his hands. These blasts are strong enough to produce basketball-sized holes in the ground. To Gida it looked as though his attacks were connecting due to the explosions, but upon closer inspection the blasts were going right through the Shadows.

"Darn, not working huh? If my energy attacks aren't working, then I know my punches and kicks will be just as ineffective." Gida thought to himself as he realized his attacks did nothing more than attract the attention of the Shadows to him.

"You guys are tough...good. Then try THIS!" Gida shouted as he jumped onto the wall and used it as a foothold.

He then jumped out the window and onto the roof of another building. Gida looked at the horizon, he probably only had five minutes of sunlight left. That's more than enough time.

Gida closed his eyes and began absorbing sunlight, creating a yellow haze around his body. He drowned out the noises the Shadows were making as he focused. Once Gida opened his eyes, he caused the sunlight he absorbed in his body to solidify. A one-foot long, sharp, yellow crystal grew out of the palm of Gida's right hand which he clutched onto. He brought his right arm across his body, preparing to throw the crystal, but he halted as he witnessed something. He saw an NGA soldier die but that's not what stopped him, it was how the soldier died. One of the Shadow Reapers fired a bolt of energy into the man. This man died from the inside out. It didn't harm him physically but rather his... soul!

"I've got just the form to deal with these guys. To beat them I need to overpower their soul energy attacks with an attack just like it. They say, 'you can't fight fire with fire' well here I beg to differ." Gida says as he throws the crystal at ¼ the speed of sound (192 mph) through one of the Shadow Reapers.

The crystal stuck in the ground and began to glow. Gida had five seconds before that crystal exploded. He jumped into the mass of Shadows as his body began to glow black. His power rose higher and higher until it became undetectable. He closed his eyes and began focusing. Just as a Shadow Reaper was about to attack him, the crystal exploded releasing sunlight into the proximity. The Shadow Reapers wailed and screeched as they were temporarily blinded. Then, suddenly a black lightning bolt struck Gida from the sky through the ceiling. This bolt of lightning pushed the Shadow Reapers back into their respective sectors.

Inside the smoke, black sparks of energy can be seen going off around Gida's silhouette. When the smoke cleared, the Shadow Reapers could see Gida's new form. He is now wearing a long white gown with black squiggly lines, crosses, and skulls on it. White pants cover his legs, and two heads that look just like his are on his shoulders. A yellowish gold head is on his left shoulder. A purplish black one on his right shoulder. On the back of the gown there are two swords which he has dubbed his, "Death Swords". The swords are three feet long and are covered in a flaming black aura that is neither hot nor flames. It's simply a unique aura. Gida's left eye is now yellowish gold and his right one is purplish black. This is Gida's fourth form, his Death Form.

In the middle room they were all in, the Shadow Reapers scattered in and around the room grouped up. A line of twenty of them hovered above the floor in the large lobby room that was about the same size and height as a school gym. The first ten rapidly fired out Shadow Bolts from their hands, howling like ghosts. These attacks were just like the ones that delivered death to NGA soldiers' souls in 1-3 shots. Considering Gida was a powerful fighter and no ordinary human, perhaps this would attack the aura around his soul and deplete it before doing damage to his spirit and will.

That leaves ten Shadow Reapers left. Three of the ten were just like the ones currently firing but would not attack. However, they rose higher above the floor to increase their distance to be safer from Gida's reach. The three of them together started to form a giant black orb of Shadow Energy. The orb growing in Spirit Energy and energy that feeds off the shadows around. The darkness and shadows behind physical structures like walls and people, start to scatter and become semi three-dimensional in order to be sucked in by this giant orb high above the ground and near the ceiling.

Finally, the other seven Shadow Reapers remain. These seven were different in appearance as they were taller, around 6'5. They appear more three-dimensional and physical, however; they possessed higher spirit pressure and wield scythes. Two of them guarded the door that is straight ahead of Gida since his arrival to the fort's main lobby. The other five simply circle around rather slowly. Waiting for Gida's response to the first ten Shadow Reapers. They even vanish and reappear using Shadow Step to display their impressive speed as mere servants of the stronger Shadow Reapers they worked for. This was an attempt to confuse and make Gida flinch to be unfocused.

Gida looked around at the line of Shadow Reapers. With the current level Gida is at, everything and everyone appeared to be moving in slow motion. Gida realized this as he noticed the Shadow Reapers were hovering slowly. Suddenly, Gida felt a surge of energy come from the Shadow Reapers. He looked up and saw ten of the Shadow Reapers firing Shadow Bolts from their hands. Like their movements, this attack was also traveling in slow motion to Gida. This gave him enough time to analyze the attack which seemed very familiar. Ah, it was the same attack that killed an NGA trooper from the inside out. Gida decided it was best to avoid this lethal attack.

He said just one word, "Reflection".

This command caused the yellowish gold head's eyes to flash. This flash caused a yellowish gold barrier to surround Gida's entire body. The Shadow Bolts hit the barrier and ricocheted off it in all directions at ½ the speed of sound (384 mph). Some of the bolts rebound back and hit the Shadow Reapers who fired them. Others hit the walls, ceiling, floor, and doors. After successfully defending against the Shadow Reapers' attacks, Gida's barrier fades away and he takes out his Death Swords. Gida's black aura with gold lightning bolts accompanying it erupts from his body as he dashes towards the Shadow Reapers at the speed of sound (767 mph) with his Death Swords pointing outwards. His Death Swords phase through four of the Shadow Reapers' bodies, causing them to get very weak and sluggish. This occurred because of Gida's Death Energy. This energy absorbs souls, instantly killing anyone it pierces. This energy is different than natural energy or any other form of energy since this energy absorbs life. Since this energy doesn't act like natural energy, Gida can never run out of it or exhaust himself. As long as Gida is alive, his cells will continue supplying Death Energy to his body. His Death Energy, which is surrounding his swords, causes anyone or anything to get ill, weak, or ten years older.

After attacking these Shadow Reapers, Gida turns his attention towards the three Shadow Reapers who are hovering off the ground. Gida squints as he watched these three Reapers form a giant black orb of energy. This black orb began to grow and suck in shadows all over the room. Although, since it was almost nighttime, the orb wouldn't get too big due to the lack of shadows present in the room. However, Gida's attention shifted towards the last seven Shadow Reapers in the room. These Shadow Reapers were bigger, possessed weapons, and were significantly stronger than the rest of the group. Gida got distracted by these Shadow Reapers and ended up turning his back on the rest of the group. He kept his eyes on the fast-moving Shadow

Reapers. Although they were moving fast, to Gida their movements were easy to follow.

The large Shadow Orb up high in the room is fully charged. Despite there being little shadows due to not much light around, they were still there and would still exist to be enough for the three Shadow Reapers. The orb gave off a small flash that manifests a dark purple light in the center of it, now appearing to look like it was glass or something electromagnetic. Just like the Shadow Bolts Gida saw, this attack is of the same nature. It primarily targeted the souls of the living with very little physical damage. The orb starts to fall at the acceleration of gravity (9.8 meters per second) like it had physical mass. This attack should be noted to still be energy based.

As the orb falls to the ground, the other Shadow Reapers didn't wait for it to land. The four Shadow Reapers were all struck by the Death Swords and three of them were hit in critical areas. One of them died as he withered into a pile of Shadow Feathers that soon faded away. The other three were staggered. The fourth one backed away slowly and the others that were not touched at all hovered away to gain distance from Gida. The five S2 Shadow Reapers with higher presences and with scythes finally attacked. The first one flew down to swing widely at Gida with his scythe. The scythe is semi-physical and can pierce through skin and even bone to draw out blood. Additionally, a shadowy aura engulfed the blade of the scythe temporarily whenever ANY of the S2 Shadow Reapers swung. This swing was horizontal from right to left in a hooking motion; a movement that is suited for a scythe fighting style.

The other four swooped in at a much faster and sudden pace using Shadow Step. They took their positions swiftly in front of one another and suddenly appeared, attacking. The second S2 Shadow Reaper swung downward, like a hammer slamming into a nail, towards Gida's right shoulder. The third swinging upward in a sweeping motion in attempt to hook Gida or cleave his chest and jaw vertically to send him back. The fourth performing an upward diagonal swing to the left. The fifth performing an upward diagonal swing to the right. At the end of the combo, all five S2 Shadow Reapers swung relatively at the same time if not most of them. They all moved up together to cover Gida in a 270-degree angle leaving him only the 90-degree opening to move back. All of them swung horizontally both in a wide and narrow manner collectively. They also swung in different directions collectively, left or right, a formation that can only be performed as a group. An individual obviously cannot realistically swing both right and left. This final attack of the combo involving all five Shadow Reapers would target all five zones of Gida's body. His head, left chest/arm, right chest/arm, left leg, and right leg.

If Gida chooses to evade for the most part, especially towards the end, Gida will be at the area where the large Shadow Orb from above lands. The orb, upon physical or spiritual contact, will shatter and explode immediately. This releases a highly concentrated explosion of the Shadow Reaper's Spirit/Shadow Energy that marks everything physical including the walls and floor in mystical black energy. This energy tears away nearby souls of living beings other than Shadow Reapers. The Shadow Reapers themselves are immune. This is much more powerful and widespread than a Shadow Reaper's simple Shadow Bolt. The explosion appears to be electromagnetic energy rather than fiery energy, leaving those after the explosion to contain electrical charges engulfing them slightly. To normal human like beings, this would kill them like a bomb on the spiritual plane. To higher beings like Gida, this damages their soul or weakens their aura. This damages their spirit energy reserves a significant amount as well.

Gida's attention shifts back to the orb of energy once it gives off the small flash.

"Tch..." Gida spits in disgust as he realizes he forgot about the orb previously.

He notices the orb is falling to the ground rather slowly (since Gida is so fast now) and squints his eyes. Before he can say or do a thing referencing the orb, Gida suddenly feels a disturbance in the air. Gida turns back around to see one of the high-level Shadow Reapers flying towards him. Once the Reaper was close enough, he swung his scythe widely at Gida. Gida smiled as he could vividly follow the Reaper's movements. He decided to test the power behind this Reaper's attack, so Gida put the Death Sword in his left hand up beside his face. The tip of the sword was pointing straight up. Gida anticipated for his Death Sword to intercept the blade of the scythe, stopping it. However, due to the length of the Reaper's arms and the width of which he swung; the Death Sword intercepted it around the middle portion of the scythe. This caused the blade portion of the scythe to keep going, scratching Gida's cheek.

"These guys have the reach advantage on me, I better be cautious. Especially since those weapons aren't normal." Gida thinks to himself as he backs away from the Reaper.

At the same time he begins backing away, unknowingly heading towards the orb, the other Reapers swoop in ready to attack. It was a little harder for Gida to keep up with these Reapers, since they increased their speed.

Gida watched as these four landed in front of one another and dashed in front of him. He dodged the first blow by turning his upper body 90 degrees to the right, causing the scythe to miss and instead slam into the ground. He dodged the next one by jumping backwards four feet, staying out of range of the scythe that tried to impale his chest and jaw. Seeing both Reapers attack him at once, Gida decides to again block the attack. He puts both of his Death Swords straight up in front of him. This causes the scythes to slam into them rather than Gida. However, the combined power between the Reapers slides Gida back four feet. Making him four feet closer to the descending orb. After stopping himself and looking up, Gida realizes he is surrounded.

"These guys are pretty good." Gida thinks to himself as he looks around at the Reapers who prepare to attack again.

Gida witnesses the Reapers all attack him and he jumps backwards another four feet, dodging the blows. However, he jumps back right into the orb.

The orb, upon contact with Gida, explodes on him. This explosion launches Gida through the crowd of Reapers and into a wall at ½ the speed of sound, leaving a hole. His black aura with gold lightning bolts vanished during the explosion, allowing him to sustain damage mainly from the hard crash into the wall. As Gida lays inside the wall, he can't help but notice he is a little weaker than before. No matter though, he has more than enough power to fend off these Reapers.

"That one hurt a bit. Time to get serious." Gida thinks to himself as he gets out of the hole and stands up.

"Separate!" Gida commands.

This causes the two heads on his shoulders to detach and form their own bodies. One yellowish gold and the other purplish black. These other Gidas are clones of the original. All three Gidas look up at the Shadow Reapers, preparing to attack. This is Gida's ultimate move, Trinity Attack, so we will see how the Reapers fare against it. Fighting one Gida is hard enough, well now the Reapers must contend against three.

Chapter Three

One of the S2 Shadow Reapers raises his arm gesturing to the rest of the Shadow Reapers in the room. All the Shadow Reapers, except the two S2 Shadow Reapers guarding the door, go to the next room. All the S1 Shadow Reapers begin firing Shadow Bolts at Gida, even the three close to the ceiling. Of the five S2 Shadow Reapers, two of them went for the yellowish gold Gida clone, a different two Shadow Step over to the dark purple clone, and the one who just gave the command would Shadow Step three consecutive times in a zigzag motion to confuse Gida. The Shadow Reaper's pattern is left, right, right. The Shadow Reaper plants his right foot down, lunging forward and swinging his scythe at Gida with swift force. The scythe is used like a spear/lance, where the rod of the scythe was held with one hand, but the hand acted as its own inward force to the left. While the back end of the rod was against his ribs, pushing outward. This acts as a lever that allows enough mechanical efficiency to land a strong strike towards Gida's side. Not only due to the technique of the scythe being swung, but also the rotation of the hips as the Shadow Reaper swings. Ideally this was also due to his initial footing after the Shadow Step.

The four Shadow Reapers that went after the two clones rapidly swing diagonally left and right and occasionally up and down in a barrage of strikes. They attempted to remain fast and offensive regardless of there being any openings. From the side view it looked like wheels of black and purple from the motion path the Shadow Reapers used and how fast they were swinging. The four S2 Shadow Reapers' goal was to essentially overwhelm the clones and force them to remain defensive, not having a chance to attack. Additionally, there were the Shadow Bolts coming from the line of S1 Shadow Reapers.

The three Gidas stare confidently at the Reapers as they prepared their attacks. They all watch as the S1 Reapers fired Shadow Bolts at the original Gida. Remembering the Shadow Orb he was just struck by, Gida decides to destroy these bolts and the Reapers. He pointed his right hand up at the three Reapers floating in the air and pointed his left hand at the remaining Reapers in the room. Two black balls of Death Energy begin forming in front of his hands. These energy balls are the size of his hands. Gida then fires two beams of Death Energy at ½ the speed of sound towards the Reapers and their Shadow Bolts. Gida's beams completely overwhelmed the Shadow Reapers' attacks since his beams can destroy 26% of a planet each. That is all of Australia, Oceania, Europe, Antarctica, and 50% of South America combined. After eliminating the Shadow Bolts, the beams completely engulf the S1 Reapers before exploding on them in a black cloud of smoke. This attack should completely eradicate the Reapers due to the potency of Death Energy present in the beams. If they somehow managed to survive these beams, then they will succumb to the cloud of smoke engulfing them. Since this smoke is the remnant of the beams, it too is Death Energy. After this attack, Gida focused on the one high-level Reaper approaching him.

"Attack!" Gida commands.

This command causes his two clones to glow their respective colors before dashing towards their own Reapers at 3/5 the speed of light (402,369,977 mph). Moving this fast makes it seem like the clones vanished and then reappeared in front of their group of Reapers. Why? That's because the clones have entered and exited the Hyper-Speed Realm. The Hyper-Speed Realm is a realm that contains beings and objects that move at speeds close to or exactly at their full speed. In this realm the objects and beings essentially do not exist in the real world. This allows none of the factors in the real world to affect them. If a fight were to take place in this realm, the two fighters would be moving in slow motion when really, in the real world, they are moving at high speeds.

As Gida watched the slow-moving S2 Reaper begin his attack, he began thinking.

"This one must be the boss, if I restrain him, I may be able to control this fight." Gida thinks to himself just as the Reaper begins swinging his scythe again.

Not in the mood to play around with this Shadow Reaper, Gida glowed black and dashed at 3/5 the speed of light to the right then behind this Reaper, vanishing. Once behind him, Gida reappeared and leaned his head back, avoiding the follow-through of the Reaper's swing. After the Reaper's attack was finished, Gida quickly put the Death Sword in his right hand close to the Reaper's throat. He then turned so he and the Reaper would be watching Gida's clones be on the defensive from their onslaught of Reapers attacking them.

"Halt!"

Gida shouts out startling all the Reapers and his own clones. "Surrender this fight or this one dies." Gida demands and shows he is serious by pressing his Death Sword into the Reaper's neck a little.

This pause in the battle was enough for the clones to finally take the offensive. They pointed both of their hands at their group of

Reapers. Two balls of Death Energy, in their respective colors, form in front of their hands. These energy balls are the size of their hands. The yellowish gold Gida had yellowish gold balls of Death Energy and the purplish black one had purplish black ones. However, they did not fire. In this predicament the Reapers were trapped. If any of them dared make a sudden move, they would be blasted by Gida's clones. If they failed to surrender, then the lead of the Reapers would be killed alongside his troops from the blasts. What will the Reapers do now?

Everything that Gida and his clones had done was successful. The ones attacked by beams died in an instant; the smoke of Death Energy was almost unnecessary. The remaining Shadow Reapers stood surprised and silent when the sword was put to their Squad Captain's neck. However, the S2 Shadow Reaper having Gida's sword by his neck would still be holding his scythe. The scythe shattered into Shadow Energy then reformed at lightning speed (220,000,000 mph) into chains of Limbo. The Shadow Chains were already floating and wrapped in a ring that surrounded both the S2 Shadow Reaper and Gida. The chains quickly decreased their distance apart from each other and closed in to wrap tightly around Gida and the S2 Shadow Reaper, trapping them. They were bound both physically and spiritually as the chains bound both their souls. Obviously, this was suicide but for greater results. The Shadow Reapers resumed their fire of Shadow Bolts, primarily at Gida. They ignored the clones completely at this moment.

The two S2 Shadow Reapers guarding the door strayed away from their duties as guards and helped their fellow Shadow Reapers tend to the enemy who has proven to be more troublesome as time continues. They vanished into the darkness and reappeared elsewhere. Specifically, they came right out of the shadows of Gida's clones who were energy based and thus produced light to reveal shadows on them. The two S2 Shadow Reapers rising from Gida's clones' shadows also ignored the clones. They all approached Gida to strike him from the left and right; swinging down and approaching him all in the same speed, the speed of Shadow Step; being half of lightning speed (110,000,000 mph).

The blades of their scythes were engulfed by Shadow Flame enchantments.

Gida looked around at all the Shadow Reapers while holding his Death Sword to the captain's neck. The entire time he was doing this, Gida forgot about the scythe which turned into chains. The sudden appearance of the chains caught Gida off guard who didn't have time to avoid them. Being pressed this close to the Reaper caused Gida's Death Sword to press completely into the Reaper's neck, killing him. As the Shadow Reapers fired their Shadow Bolts, Gida's clones fired their beams at the Reapers. These beams are strong enough to destroy 26% of a planet each. The Reapers were eradicated but not before their Shadow Bolts struck Gida and the already dead S2 Reaper.

"Agh!" Gida cries out in pain as he gets struck by the Shadow Bolts.

He falls to one knee with the limp and dead S2 Shadow Reaper attached to him.

As Gida's clones were firing their devastating beams, they did not notice the two S2 Reapers behind them. The clones dissipate after firing their beams, leaving the bound Gida to deal with the two remaining S2 Reapers. As the Reapers moved at their speeds, Gida looked up, much weaker than he started off. This is due to the Shadow Bolts and the Shadow Orb that struck him before. Rendered helpless, Gida was struck by the scythes of the two Reapers, causing him to cough out blood. He painfully looked down at his wounds before glaring at the two Reapers in front of him. Gida returned to his Base Form before he began glowing gold.

Chapter Four

Suddenly, a gold lightning bolt struck Gida through the roof of the building. This lightning bolt either eradicates or pushes the Reapers, along with their scythes, away from Gida. Inside the smoke, gold flickers of energy can be seen going off around Gida's silhouette. Gida stands up completely as the smoke fades away revealing his new form. His shirt disintegrated, revealing his toned and muscular body. His eyes are glowing gold, his pants are gold, and his shoes are gold. This is Gida's fifth form, his Universal Form.

In this form he is 50x stronger than he just was.

"This is my Universal Form, to be honest I didn't think I was going to have to use it." Gida says.

The rest of the Shadow Reapers were destroyed by Gida's clones' blasts. The blasts were quite powerful and beyond the Shadow Reapers' power. The two S2 Shadow Reapers were caught off guard after they assumed they had landed critical injuries to Gida. They were blasted away by the sheer force and power of the lightning that empowers Gida and marks his symbolism of the universe. The S2 Shadow Reapers were blown away and ripped apart like black fabrics. They then converted back to the second dimension as shadows. These shadows withered away due to them being outshined by Gida's light. All the Shadow Reapers in the room are dead.

The double doors, wood and metal, in front of Gida at the other end of the room remained closed. Whatever presence the door embodied or what lies behind it seemed to be more noticeable with all the Shadow Reapers near Gida gone. There were obviously more, and among them were the ones that are stronger.

Gida senses something powerful emanating from behind those doors. He can't help but smile. He puts his right hand down to his wounds and is surprised to see they have healed so fast.

This is a perk of being a Mutant; regenerative capabilities. The only way to nullify these capabilities is to have some foreign Death Energy enter Gida's body via the wound. Luckily for him, these Reapers do not possess Death Energy. Wishing to save his energy and realizing going into his Universal Form was a bit too much, Gida powers down to his Base Form. He approaches the double doors and uses his physical strength to push open the doors. Whatever or whoever was on the other side, Gida was ready to face them.

Chapter Five

When Gida opened the doors, he could see a hall that was far darker than the room he was just in. Almost hard to see. There were dark purple flames on each side of the hall, like lit candles, but they did not give off enough light to make the room any brighter. However, at the end of the hall, it was a little less dark. It was bright enough for Gida to at least see that there was someone standing at the end of the hall. This dark figure simply walked away into the other hall that continues at the end of this hall. The presence behind the door seemed to have become weaker. Or perhaps it was not there to begin with. Gida would feel things have become empty. The hall was closed off from the whole world.

Although Gida was essentially blind for the first part of the hall, he could still sense that strange powerful presence in the room. As he progressed down the hall, he began to see what looks like the makings of some being. Just as his eyes began to adjust however, the being left. Now alone, Gida could hear everything inside his body flowing, moving, and beating. It was rather deafening how quiet it was. It was too quiet, the type of quiet that makes you feel like you aren't alone or that you're being watched. Gida scanned the room for any power signals but found none. So, he pressed on in the direction the being went.

When Gida made it to the end of the hall, there was a different hall around that corner to the right. Gida still saw darkness and nothing but purple candle lights that did not help. However, like the other hall, there was a bit more light coming from the other end of the hall that probably led to another hall. Still very dark, one of the purple flame lit candles flickered. The light of the flame being completely blocked out as if someone in the dark had just walked past it, blocking Gida's view. This black figure seemed to be walking away from Gida. This happened again two seconds later at a farther candlelight.

Once Gida saw the flickering candles, he got a bit perturbed.

"Enough games. Hya!" Gida shouts as a gold lightning bolt strikes him from the sky through the building.

When the smoke settles, he is back in his Universal Form. This time however, his gold aura with gold energy hands is lighting up the entire room allowing him to finally see. Now being able to see, Gida looked around.

"Come on out. I know you're there, no sense in hiding anymore." Gida says to the figure as he continues looking around.

Nothing. With the room lit up, the hall was empty. As a matter of fact, it would seem to still be dark. It was as if the walls and ceiling of the hall were black, just making everything darker in general. Whoever made the candle lights flicker is no longer there. Rather, at the end of the hall, instead of it being lighter, it was darker.

Now in his Universal Form, Gida meant business. He ran to the end of the hall and around the corner, only to be met with another hall. He confidently strode down this hall, positive that nothing could harm him in this form. Once in the middle of the hall, he stopped and reverted to his Base Form, not wanting to waste power.

"Enough of this..." Gida muttered to himself as he stood in the middle of the hall with his eyes closed, heightening his senses.

He no longer was pursuing who or whatever was in the building with him, he was going to be patient and let them come to him.

While his eyes were closed, Gida began raising his power higher. Not to fight anyone but to become a signal to draw out his foes.

With the dark returning, it seemed those hiding returned as well. Moments after Gida closed his eyes, someone was coming from the end of the hall, in front of Gida, running towards him. There was no sound of footsteps running, but simply the sensation through the air and of something living approaching him. If Gida opened his eyes, it would look like the same being as before who got in the way of the candle lights.

Suddenly, there was another person at the other end of the hall behind Gida, running towards him. Gida felt as if the space in this area was simply closing in on him. Was it just the darkness or was something coming for him?

With his eyes closed, Gida could feel a presence, or was it just the pressure, closing in on him. He suddenly opened his eyes only to be greeted by more darkness. He looked around again, listening for footsteps. When he heard none, he closed his eyes again. He couldn't shake the uneasy feeling that something or someone was approaching him though. Has Gida gone mad or was something out there? He decided to play on the safe side as he assumed his fighting stance. Gida's power began raising 20x higher.

"Hya!" Gida shouted as his white aura erupted from his body producing F0 tornado winds (40-72 mph).

As soon as his aura was produced, he reopened his eyes. This time however, he was greeted by a silhouette running towards him. As his aura faded away, Gida now had his answer and remained on guard for this being. However, he was oblivious to the one behind him.

Chapter Six

Something physical manifested behind him as the being ran towards Gida. It was a sword being held in the being's hand. This happened swiftly and within three meters (10 feet) of Gida. It was less than a second when this unknown being, unidentified because of the darkness, ran past Gida with the blade following. The blade slashed into Gida's side/rib area or his arm if it was there. Just simply running through with the blade sticking out to bump into and cut anyone the being passes by. The blade was sharp enough to cleave and hack someone's armor off or cut into the bones/ ribs of someone. After this attempt, the sword seemed to disappear. In actuality, the sword had switched planes into something that isn't physical.

Gida's arm was cleaved causing him to cry out in pain.

"Agggh!" He cries out as he clutches his dangling right arm.

He winces in pain as he follows the being's movements and pursues after it, no longer caring about the one he initially saw charging towards him. As he was pursuing the being who attacked him, his right arm began to regenerate. However, Gida did not wait for it to heal completely before attacking.

"Ha!" Gida shouts as he fires a white energy beam from his left hand at ¼ the speed of sound towards the being.

This energy beam is strong enough to destroy 1% of a planet. That is 20% of Australia and Oceania combined. If the being dodges this beam, it will destroy the wall.

The being dodges the beam rather proficiently. The dodge was a mere step to the side, but the dark figure in the darkness was distorted as it left trails of shadows. This of course is the Shadow Step that the Shadow Reapers use. The Shadow Reaper turns to face Gida after the dodge. The beam destroyed a part of the wall and ceiling as lights shine through. Though not from the sun, but the night sky since it was still dark. The shining moon revealed the Shadow Reaper. The other being starts to be revealed too, but it had already gotten away as it made its turn to the other hall at the end of this hall.

"Too much power..." The Shadow Reaper said in a pale whispering voice while facing Gida.

This voice is oddly projected loud enough to be heard, even at a loud music concert. The Shadow Reaper drew out its bow before Shadow Stepping backwards to the end of the hallway at speeds equivalent to lightning. These Shadow Reapers are faster than the S2 Shadow Reapers with scythes that Gida fought earlier. An arrow was also already drawn during the time of the Shadow Step and was ready to fire.

The arrow was shot at Gida at Mach 20 (15,345 mph). The arrow was aiming towards Gida's chest and upon any contact, the arrow will first pierce through if it can, then collapse and explode in Shadow Energy expanding 10 meters (33 feet) wide. The explosion seemed slow and electromagnetic, even though it was black and forged from the abominations of the Shadow Reapers.

This attack was also on the spirit plane where it effects one's soul. The explosion that engulfed those within seemed to slowly damage the soul/Spirit Energy of the soul. It seemed binding, making those with souls stagger and find it hard to move, like moving within quicksand. From the center of the explosion, 1.5 seconds after the explosion started, a second explosion occurred. This time impacting both the spiritual and physical planes. The second explosion is purple, and specifically a totally different type of energy. This energy is ten times stronger than normal energy and is known as Chaos Energy.

Chaos Energy is one of the strongest negative energy types by nature, considering it's very strong/potent. Chaos Energy is chaotic and allows the user of this energy to invoke chaos into the world. It is an energy that is unstable and thus results in aggressive reactions such as intense explosions. Due to such, controlling this energy is difficult, as well as fending against it. Those who attempt to absorb this energy will fail to do so or go physically/mentally mad; a penalty for working with some-thing unstable. The effects of this energy are, by its very name, chaotic. With this energy, the user disturbs order and hope. Such as the power outside and inside Gida. Such effects are almost undefined and do not correlate strongly to a specific result, but that itself is one of the deadly attributes of Chaos Energy.

After firing the shot, the Shadow Reaper leaves the hall in the same manner as the other. Returning to another dark hallway.

As Gida's beam missed, he noticed it is still night outside.

"Darn..." Gida says under his breath.

He needs the sun to be able to use his attacks to their fullest capabilities. Too busy caught up in his own head, Gida did not notice the arrow being shot at him until the last moment. He gasped and crossed his arms in an X in front of him, attempting to block the arrow. The arrow pierced his arms which Gida expected, however; he did not expect the explosion to go off. This explosion blew a hole in Gida's arms and slid him backwards 50 feet before Gida stopped himself. Thinking the attack was over, Gida lowered his guard briefly and looked at his arms. This was a mistake as the second and more powerful explosion went off, sending Gida crashing through the opposite wall from the Reaper. He laid there in the rubble with blood leaking from his nose, mouth, head, and arms. He also was rendered paralyzed from the spiritual assault due to the first explosion. If the Reaper hadn't run off, Gida may have been hurt even more than he currently was. Unable to move, Gida began regenerating.

After getting back to full health, Gida got out of the rubble and walked to the hole in the wall. He stared at the moon and clenched his fists.

"I won't let you down father." Gida said to himself before his white aura erupted from his body, producing F1 tornado winds (73-112 mph).

"Haaaa!" Gida shouted as he put his clenched hands at his waist, powering up to full power in this form.

Gida indeed was sloppy in this encounter after going into his Universal Form twice and using his regenerative capabilities twice. Gida wanted to remain in his Base Form for a couple minutes as to not waste anymore power. That would be a problem with the fact that these Reapers were faster than him at this level. Since he is at full power, he can at most destroy 17% of a planet. That makes his full power attack strong enough to destroy all of Australia, Oceania, Europe, and 56% of Antarctica combined. Although Gida is in his Base Form, he is still a threat and has enough power to easily destroy one of these Reapers.

After powering up to full power, Gida turned and walked down the same dark hallway the two Reapers went down earlier.

Chapter Seven

As Gida continued down the hallway, it returns to being dark considering Gida was now walking away from the hole in the fort that made it lighter due to the moon shining through. Although it was dark again, his senses returned to their normal state. He sensed the Shadow Reapers that he just encountered, three of them. There was nothing standing in his way as he walked through the hall. However, he came to a dead end. The hall had large rocks and debris collapsed down to completely block any way through. However, there was a ten-meter-wide hole in the ground that led somewhere. If Gida decides to continue onward and jump down to get through the blocked hallway, he would fall 50 feet down to what seemed to be an underground tunnel. From there, as he continued down the tunnel, it led to a large open underground cave that is five times larger than the room he fought the weaker Shadow Reaper minions earlier. In this open area, three Shadow Reapers dressed in the same attire would be standing next to each other all facing Gida. This time they were finally going to fight Gida.

"This is as far as you will go. " The one in the middle said with a more clear and superior voice, but still distorted like a Reaper.

This one appeared to barely be armed. However, behind his back would be a medium sized dagger. His arms were crossed.

"Obviously...any effort is a risk to him if he ever wishes to stand a chance against Lord Gaelingheim and Advisor Eris." The one to the left with bows and arrows said with a dry voice.

This reaper is the one who last injured Gida. On the right was another Shadow Reaper who took a step forward with his hand reaching to his back to hold the hilt of a katana sheathed there.

Gida did indeed jump down and was greeted by an underground cave. Thankfully, this cave was a little lighter than the fort, so

Gida could look around at his surroundings. He stopped looking around once he saw the three Shadow Reapers there. Almost as if they were waiting for him.

"Aha, these were the guys I was chasing from before." Gida *thinks to himself.*

He listens to their dialogues intently while scanning their bodies for weapons.

"Lord Gaelingheim and Advisor Eris? ...Who are you, who are they, and why are you taking over this fort?" Gida *asked as his eyes locked onto the bow and arrow.*

He also saw one of the Reapers reaching behind his back. A blade of some sort most likely was there Gida concluded.

"If you do not answer me, I'll just force it out of you three. What will you be able to do now that I can see? You don't have the element of surprise anymore. I'll also tell you one thing...you and your troops are PISSING ME OFF!!!" Gida *shouts as his white aura flares up, producing F1 tornado winds.*

Now ready to fight, Gida prepared himself for the Reapers' response.

"Come on! Show me your power!" Gida demands still powered up by his white aura.

(Shadow Reaper one - dagger and adept shadow user, Shadow Reaper two - bow and arrow, Shadow Reaper three - katana that's a Starblade)

The three of them remained in silence as they didn't seem interested in talking anymore, at least not to Gida who they find inferior. When Gida's aura created pressure comparable to that of a tornado, the wind went past them and caused them to flash black and white, appearing ghost-like for that instant in time. This was due to the Shadow Reaper in the middle who manipulated the shadows of himself and his comrades. It could be seen that their shadows combined were not two-dimensional shapes of their three-dimensional and humanoid shapes. Their shadows were the shape of the sun with its flames on the edges looking like black tentacles.

The Shadow Reaper on the left quickly unsheathed his sword and began running towards Gida at Mach one speed (767 mph). An aura of Shadow Mist surrounds the Shadow Reaper holding a katana that changes its form. The blade starts to distort and look organic and not 100% straight/symmetric. There was a shadowy aura around the blade as if it was black flames. However, these flames did not possess heat. When the Shadow Reaper came as close as five meters (16 feet), he vanished. He was simply gone from that point in space. His shadow started to collapse and shrink into nothingness. This odd delay was because the shadow was not fast enough to keep up with the physical body that created that shadow. Such is this phenomenon.

Gida's shadow, however; warped into a different shape that now appeared to be two people instead of one. It was that Shadow Reaper who vanished, who was behind Gida. This is a tier one ability of the Shadow Reaper, to teleport through shadows. Upon teleporting, the Shadow Reaper continued to do what he had previously started before the warp of spacetime through shadows. The Shadow Reaper ran past Gida and back to his comrades with his sword positioned outward to cut into Gida again while running by. This attack was the same sword attack that Gida was struck by earlier in the halls. However, this time without the help of the Shadow Reaper with the ability to phase in and out of the physical plane using shadows.

"Phase through, Ketsuesugi." Shadow Reaper three murmured after performing the strike.

The sword was aimed at Gida's arm/lower rib area again. However, this time the sword was engulfed by a Shadow Aura that collided against Gida's white aura. This aura was a Dokenkai ability of the Shadow Reaper's Starblade, a weapon with a soul and thus power that is bonded with their wielder by Soul Contract. Starblades are one of the very first contracted weapons to ever exist. The very idea of contracts was invented by the Shadow Reapers. It is that fact that grants the Shadow Reapers the talent of being the strongest of Starblade users out of all the other races and clans in Mugen existence. The Dokenkai is a first release of the Starblade when the user knows its name. The Dokenkai ability named after the Starblade named "Ketsuesugi" casts an aura around its blade. This allows the blade it engulfs to go through the projected power and strike the body. This Star-blade can be simply categorized as an anti-energy weapon.

Shadow Reaper two with the bow and arrows vanished just like how Shadow Reaper three did, teleporting elsewhere. Where though?

Shadow Reaper one weaved hand signs before forming a final one with both hands. Inhaling in before exhaling out a giant fire-ball of Shadow Flames that were three-dimensional. The angle of the fireball, the size of ten meters, causes it to fly towards Gida's feet. The fireball will collide against the ground, if it misses Gida, and combust into Shadow Flames. This fireball is just as destructive and damaging as the large orb of Shadow Energy dropped onto Gida when fighting the lesser Shadow Reapers. This was due to the level of high control and technique, as well as the essence of the Shadow Energy making it reach temperatures 2,500 degrees Celsius (4,532 degrees Fahrenheit). Considering how this attack was created by only one Shadow Reaper without any charge up or absorption of the shadows around the battlefield, simply demonstrates the power level of these Shadow Reapers.

"Bring it." Gida said to the Shadow Reaper currently running towards him with his blade unsheathed.

Gida thankfully was able to keep up with this Reaper's movements since his full speed in this form is the speed of sound. As soon as Gida prepared to counter the Reaper's charge, the Reaper vanished. This act caught Gida off guard who gasps. Not even a second later, Gida feels a presence and without turning around, concludes that the Reaper is behind him with his blade still. Although he cannot see the attack coming, the aura around the blade gives off its position. Gida senses the blade and does a backflip over the charging Reaper and his blade. The blade still pierced through Gida's aura, causing it to dissipate. Gida lands 10 feet away from the Reaper just as the Reaper with the bow and arrow disappears.

Chapter Eight

As soon as Gida lands, the Reaper fires the giant fireball of Shadow Flames.

"Tch..." Gida spits.

He can already feel the heat behind this attack and knows it is too much for him. Just when things were going bad for Gida, he feels a sudden surge of power run throughout his body. Almost instantly, a black lightning bolt strikes Gida's body. Inside the smoke a voice can be heard.

"Reflection." It says.

As the ball of Shadow Flames passes through the smoke it gets rebounded back towards the Shadow Reaper. However, this time it travels at ½ the speed of sound and is strong enough to destroy 51% of the planet. That is all of Australia, Oceania, Europe, Antarctica, South America, North America, and 10% of Africa combined. Inside the smoke, Gida has transformed back into his Death Form. The reason the ball of Shadow Flames got reflected was because of the yellowish gold head on Gida's left shoulder. This head produced a barrier of the same color that reflected the attack. Not only that but upon contact with the barrier, the Shadow Fireball was flooded with Death Energy, amplifying its strength.

As the smoke clears, Gida's form is now visible to the Reapers. Gida simply puts his right hand above his head as a black ball of energy forms above his hand. This energy ball swells to 400 feet wide and tall. The size of this ball goes through the cave and fort itself, destroying multiple rooms and sections of the building before bursting out into the open. This is Gida's Death Bomb, one of his deadliest super attacks.

After forming the massive ball of energy, Gida hurls it at ½ the speed of sound towards the two Shadow Reapers. The third one is still nowhere to be found. This energy ball is filled with Death Energy, giving it its black color. Not only that, that makes this energy ball quite deadly. This energy ball is also strong enough to destroy 51% of the planet. However, if this energy ball explodes it will release the Death Energy inside it as a mist. This mist will cover 400 feet and do the same thing as Death Energy.

After launching his attack, Gida floats out of the cave, out of the ruined fort, and 400 feet into the air. Here he hovers, waiting for the Reaper's response to his attack.

The Shadow Reaper stood where he was and gazed at his own attack being slightly altered and sent back flying.

"This is enough power to destroy a city...no...more...what a waste." Shadow Reaper one muttered before Shadow Stepping to the right side of the cave to easily dodge his own attack that got reflected.

The Shadow Fireball hit the end of the cave and combusted into Shadow Flames. Shadow Reaper one now stood on the wall like it was the new ground. He used his Shadow Energy control on his feet to remain attached to the wall as he walked on it. His arms were crossed like they were before. His shadow expanded again into the shape of a black sun. The edges of his shadow start to extend and stretch along the wall to the ground. These are Shadow Strings. They moved towards Gida like snakes slithering towards him fast; traveling 300 mph each and attempting to approach Gida from different angles from his right.

Shadow Reaper three would not wait for what Shadow Reaper one plans to do with his Shadow Manipulation. Shadow Reaper three Shadow Stepped at lightning speed to get right in front of Gida at this time. Already moving to make an attack before he finished forming back into a three-dimensional being from Shadow Step. However, he was a full being right before the attack was going to land, by a few nanoseconds. Hence, the strike itself was decelerating from lightning speed and by the time it hits, it was still a relatively fast and swift strike. The sword was still engulfed in the anti-energy aura to slash at Gida's chest and ultimately cut his arm off to stop his stronger attack with Death

Energy. Shadow Reaper three hoped that the interruption of energy flowing through Gida's arm and thus the orb would cause the orb to shut down and not go off at all. If not, simply stopping him from using the orb to do a full-on attack. Obviously, the time it took to deliver a sword strike was much faster. The sword swing was of adept caliber. A foot was planted forward to make the stance a sort of lunge that was established at the end of the Shadow Step. He immediately swung his arms together in a motion that was chained to the lunge. This sword was the most qualified weapon, that can shut down Gida's attack being powered up, at the Shadow Reaper's disposal.

Shadow Reaper two is up on the ceiling as he had teleported from the shadows of his shadow, to the shadow on the ceiling made by the rock spikes and bumps of every typical cave. The Shadow Reaper's feet stuck to the ceiling using Shadow Energy control to not fall. The bow was drawn, and an arrow would be ready to fire. Three arrows are fired this time down at Gida. With gravity on their side they had greater acceleration. The initial velocities of the three arrows were the same as the arrow from before, Mach 20. The arrows will explode upon any physical or spiritual contact in the same shadowy explosion that was electromagnetic like. This was a force of shadow that encases targets in the explosion. This will stagger and stun them while inflicting Shadow Damage over time. Afterwards they will explode, releasing Chaos Energy. It should be noted that three arrows are more destructive and damaging than simply three times. Right before the arrows hit Gida, Shadow Reaper three, who is in close range with Gida to deliver the sword blows, will Shadow Step away to prevent being caught in friendly fire.

Gida, still able to maneuver, jumps 400 feet away from the approaching slithering Shadow Strings while still holding his massive energy ball. Gida ends up landing on some rubble from the destruction his energy ball caused just from forming it. Avoiding the Shadow Strings for now, Gida sets his sights on the incoming Shadow Reaper.

Although moving at impressive speed, his speed doesn't compare to Gida who can move at 3/5 the speed of light in this form. So, to Gida the Reaper was moving in slow motion and his movements were clear and easy to follow. He watched as the Reaper approached and delivered his blow. Gida concluded that it would be difficult to fend against the blow laced in the aura while forming his energy ball. He needed help.

"Separate." Is all he says, commanding the two heads on his shoulders to detach and form their own bodies in their respective colors.

These two other Gidas are standing on each side of Gida.

The yellowish gold Gida jumps in front of the real Gida and stops the Reaper's blade with his own Death Sword laced in Death Energy. Upon contact with the Reaper's blade, the Death Energy around the clone's Death Sword dissipates. This is due to the anti-energy surrounding the Reaper's blade. Although the Death Sword is aura-less, the clone is still exponentially stronger than the Reaper. This strength allows his Death Sword to withstand the Reaper's blow and not budge or get cut through.

The purplish black Gida glows purplish black before jumping towards the incoming arrows, at 3/5 the speed of light, essentially vanishing. Once three feet away from the arrows, this clone re-appears and takes out both of his Death Swords, slashing all three of the arrows. However, he did not anticipate the arrows exploding. This explosion knocks the Death Swords out of the clone's hands and sends him flying back 400 feet at ½ the speed of sound. He crashes into some loose rubble, sending debris everywhere. Although wounded, he successfully took care of the arrows. At this moment, the Reaper clashed with the yellowish gold clone Shadow Steps away.

"They put up a good fight, but it's over now." Gida thinks to himself as he hurls the massive energy ball at the Reapers at ½ the speed of sound.

Having evaded the Reapers' attacks, this energy ball should connect unless they have more tricks up their sleeves.

Chapter Nine

Gida's explosion went off. The blackness of the explosion makes it too dark and unclear whether the Shadow Reapers survived. However, in terms of distance and position, they were indeed caught in the explosion whether they survived or not. It was dark again, perhaps darker than it normally was with the Death Mist created by the explosion. From the large shadows on the ground, black colored gale winds can be seen traveling out of them and pushing away the Death Mist. The mist is being blown away by Shadow Energy in the form of wind. From this large shadow, two Shadow Reapers rose up and appeared ghost-like before appearing physical and three-dimensional again. It was Shadow Reaper one and three. They were unharmed. Shadow Reaper three was already in the motion of escaping after his attempt to strike, regardless of success or failure.

Shadow Reaper three had Shadow Stepped back to being next to Shadow Reaper one who had the greater control of shadows and manipulated shadows in a way that masks them. Just like in those dark hallways that messed with Gida's senses. By bending shadows to mask them in this way, there was no presence, and this was due to how they literally did not exist on the third dimension. Shadow Reaper one can bend himself into a shadow that resides on a two-dimensional world. Like shadows, their physical and spiritual existence was gone. They had become literal shadows that cannot be harmed. Like the ways that shadows in the real world cannot be harmed. This of course only worked with shadows around the area. Its weakness would have to be something that could directly affect shadows. For instance, antimatter could destroy all matter, but does not destroy shadows. Light however can outshine the shadows and make them disappear. If death was in the form of light, this was a direct kill to shadows. While death in the form of a mist would not affect shadows because mist could not affect shadows in the first place, unless it gave off light.

The two Shadow Reapers hid in existing shadows while not only being masked by them. The gale winds were sent out of their shadows on the ground to make the Death Mist go away for a 50-meter (164 feet) proximity. Hopefully, this keeps the Death Mist away for the entire fight or at least for now if the mist were to come back to close the gap in the air the Shadow Reapers had made. They then rose and appeared ghost-like, still under the influence of Shadow Reaper one's ability to mask them into being shadows that could not be detected and phase through many things. They appeared physical and visible in the darkness.

Shadow Reaper one was right behind Gida's clone that blocked Shadow Reaper three's attack. Shadow Reaper one having Shadow Tendrils that physically existed through Shadow Energy. These tendrils extruded out of the Shadow Reaper's back and swiftly wrapped around to tie and trap the Gida clone in front of Gida. After trapping the clone, two more tendrils extended out and rammed at the speed of sound into the clone's head and chest, attempting to pierce through the clone's brain and heart, if it had one. The tendrils seemed to be able to do this both on the physical and spiritual plane, but only both, not one of the two. The tendrils have the force and energy to pierce though steel.

Shadow Reaper three appeared behind the real Gida, already having his Starblade ready. He attacked with jabs at high speeds and rapid rates. He performed a special technique using Shadow Step to focus its use onto the arm and side down to the waist, making those areas of the body be partially shadow and move at lightning speeds. Moving at this speed at close range causes Gida to react with less time available. The strikes were precise and fast, jabbing 30-50 times per second each at lightning speed. The retreat of the blade was slower than lightning speed. The combo lasted six seconds, landing 180 to 300 stab strikes all over Gida's body from behind. Additionally, Shadow Reaper three's blade was covered in the aura of anti-energy to pierce through Gida's aura or anything energy based to defend him. Due to this aura, the attack appeared like black energy beams rapidly firing out of his hand due to how fast the Kenjutsu strikes were being performed.

Shadow Reaper two fell from the ceiling as a corpse that was covered in decay, having been caught in the explosion. He did not have enough time or preparation to Shadow Step back to Shadow Reaper one for safety.

"Darkness, that's all I see." Gida thinks to himself as he surveys the area.

His clone in front of him also scans the area to see what damage Gida's attack did to the Reapers. When they feel a sudden wind and see some of the mist get blown away in a certain area, they know the Reapers survived. Gida's clone was completely oblivious to the fact that one of the Reapers was right behind him. He quickly got bound by the tendrils, unable to move. He looked behind himself and saw the Reaper. Gida saw his clone get bound, and jumped 400 feet backwards, next to his other clone who is still buried in the rubble. At this point Gida's clone gets stabbed in very precise locations and goes limp. The clone dissipates, leaving one more clone and the real Gida left.

Gida decides to check on his last clone which was a big mistake. He felt a presence behind him and turned around to see the other Reaper attacking him ferociously with his blade. Gida, still faster than the Reaper, was forced to bob and weave against the Reaper's assault. He was successfully dodging the Reaper's attacks while his clothes got scratched or cut a little every now and then. This was because of the Reaper's aura being able to penetrate through Gida's aura.

After the Reaper's attack, Gida flew 400 feet up into the air while rapidly firing out black energy blasts with gold lightning bolts accompanying them from his hands at ½ the speed of sound. These energy blasts are as big as his hand and have enough power to make a basketball-sized hole in the ground each. Since he fired around 25-50 of them, that's what makes them overwhelming. At the same time Gida did this, his other clone burst out of the rubble and attempted to slash the Reaper's body with his Death Swords. The real Gida stayed up in the air observing this. As he looked at the Reapers, he saw one of them fall limply from the ceiling of some rubble, most likely dead. Gida concluded that his Death Bomb was the result of that Reaper's death. Gida remained floating in the sky watching the Reaper's reactions to the attacks.

Shadow Reaper three reactively used his Shadow Step to move back a bit and at a lower speed, considering the lack of preparation. Doing so, this allowed him to dodge some of the blasts of energy, as well as give him more time to prepare a defense against the ones he could not dodge. The Shadow Reaper, wielding his Starblade, swung around and wove into block positions to reflect away and block against the attacks. The full force of the attacks not being fully asserted onto the Shadow Reaper considering his Starblade still had the ability to nullify anything energy based. The Reaper possessed formidable speed and reflexes with a block accuracy of 70%. The other 30% were barely on point and sometimes were not positioned in the right angle due to how fast Gida was firing. Additionally, not all the blocks were effective blocks, as some of the blasts would get through to damage the Shadow Reaper's armor and stamina. Eventually, this became too much for Shadow Reaper three. Luckily, Shadow Reaper one after killing the Gida clone, Shadow Stepped behind Gida and slightly above him by a 10-meter distance. The Shadow Reaper hovers with a slim aura of Shadow Energy around himself. His arms were crossed as his aura extended out the same Shadow Tendrils that stretched out at quick rates to all wrap around and pierce into Gida from behind. He attacked Gida in the same manner as Gida's clone, assuming this technique will work against the real Gida as well. None the less if this works, this would at least distract Gida and stop him early before finishing his attack on Shadow Reaper three. This will give Shadow Reaper three more time and a small break before having to deal with Gida's other clone.

Shadow Reaper three turns around seeing the last Gida clone bursting out of the rubble and approaching him with its Death Swords. The Shadow Reaper moves with matching velocities using Shadow Step and swung in the same motion the Gida clone did to have their blades clash against each other perfectly with equal force, momentum, and energy. The aura around the Starblade was kept up to cancel out the death properties of the clone's swords during that swing. The Shadow Reaper dashes back before jumping forward in a lunge to come crashing back down onto the Gida clone, swinging his Starblade down with force that is amplified due to gravity. This produced an increase in force to aid the slamming down swing onto Gida's clone. This was aimed to cut the clone's head in half vertically and cleave into his chest. Still, the aura of anti-energy engulfed the blade.

"Hyaa hya hyaa!!" Gida shouts as he continues firing his energy blasts at the Shadow Reaper.

He sees the Shadow Reaper getting overwhelmed which makes him determined to finish the assault. However, before Gida can finish, the black Shadow Tendrils wrap around him. At that moment he has a flashback of what happened to his clone, so he knows something is about to pierce him.

"Reflection!" Gida shouts which causes his yellowish gold head's eyes to flash, producing a yellowish gold barrier around Gida's body.

This barrier cuts through the tendrils wrapped around Gida's body. It also covers his body just in time as it reflects the tendrils trying to stab Gida. These tendrils get launched back at the Reaper at ½ the speed of sound. After reflecting the Reaper's attacks, Gida's barrier fades away. As Gida turns around towards the Reaper, black energy with gold lightning bolts accompanying it surrounds his right hand.

"I've got no choice, have to use another finishing move." Gida thinks to himself as he awaits the Reaper's move.

Gida's final clone is embraced in a heated one on one sword fight with the other Reaper. The clone sees the Reaper dash towards him, intending to cleave his head and chest in two. Gida's clone glows purplish black before dashing to the left at 3/5 the speed of light, vanishing and dodging the Reaper's slash. As he is gaining distance from the Reaper, the clone reappears and points his left hand towards the Reaper, firing a purplish black energy beam at him. This beam travels at ½ the speed of sound and is strong enough to destroy 26% of the planet. If this beam hits the Reaper, he most likely will be obliterated.

Shadow Reaper three saw the clone attempting a long-range attack when it had moved away to gain distance. The beam coming towards the Shadow Reaper at ½ the speed of sound was not all that astonishing in terms of speed. Though the power itself was far beyond the power reserves of the Shadow Reaper's powers. The Shadow Reaper readied himself as he got in a stance before rushing forward at the beam with his sword pointed out aligned with his shoulder. While the right hand held the blade tightly, the other hand was at the back of the hilt to push the blade forward to give it extra force to pierce through. The Shadow Reaper rushed at the beam using Shadow Step to move far beyond sound and closer to that of lightning speed. The Shadow Reaper rammed through the beam while remaining in the stance with the blade held close to pierce through while running forward. The Starblade released its maximum power at this state. This used most of its Spirit Shadow Energy to increase the strength of the anti-energy aura. The aura being thick enough to not only help the blade cut through the beam, but essentially defuse the energy of the beam from being strong enough to even damage the Shadow Reaper significantly. By the time the beam ends/when the energy is defused, the Shadow Reaper had pierced through it all to be right in front of the Gida clone. The beam perhaps being in the way of the clone's eyesight and thus not seeing this coming. Right after piercing through the beam, the Shadow Reaper continued rushing forward with the same motion. This time using his left hand to push the blade forward to thrust swiftly, forcibly stabbing into the clone's chest. Considering the blade still has a bit of its aura even after the beam, this causes the blade to cut off the power of the clone as well. Since the clone was made of energy, this causes the clone to defuse. This shuts off the clone's power, killing him.

Shadow Reaper one vanished before his reflected attack connected. He Shadow Warped as his shadow behind him had a delay in it, vanishing right after he vanished. A split second later, just like the other Shadow Reapers have performed, he teleported through a shadow in the area. Shadow Reaper one teleported right in front of Gida, facing the direction of the shadow this time. However, like last time, his shadow first distorts before forming the shadow of the Shadow Reaper. Then the Shadow Reaper appears. This delay was not much time, however. Shadow Reaper one immediately thrusts his hand forward upon teleporting, aiming his jab at Gida's face. Following the punch done in a very swift and precise manner, another punch from his other hand follows when recoiling his first fist. This time aimed at the biceps/ inner arm areas of Gida. The Shadow Reaper then steps closer and while taking the step, this allowed the Shadow Reaper to bend his arm to immediately follow with an elbow to the other arm of Gida. This blow was also aimed at his inner upper arm to take out his strength. Though this time this blow caused more severe damage and pain. The Shadow Reaper had an aura of his own to match the strength of Gida. Though this aura was not activated until performing the elbow strike and being up close to Gida where his forearm would essentially be touching against Gida's chest. From the release, and then the shove of his forearm pushing against him, this released a strong force of both physical and spiritual pressure. Shadow Reaper one had been using Shadow

Powers throughout this entire encounter. That does not mean he is lacking in other areas of combat though. Shadow Reaper one is an expert in MMA, Wing Chün, and Karate. With his smaller and slender build, compared to Gida's larger and athletic build, Shadow Reaper one uses that advantage to not only maximize his capabilities through Wing Chün, but also giving him such room to deliver these inner strikes to Gida's arms at close quarters.

The clone indeed was not expecting the Shadow Reaper to pierce through his beam. At the last moment, when the Reaper revealed itself, the clone gasped. Instead of being offensive or defensive, the clone froze out of shock before ultimately being struck by the Reaper's blade. The clone slowly dissipated as he died.

As Gida readied another ultimate attack, he saw the Shadow Reaper vanish. Like his clone, when the Reaper appeared right in front of Gida, he gasped. Rather than being defensive or offensive he was surprised. The first jab from the Shadow Reaper struck Gida. Although the power behind the punch was weak it still did its job to set up other moves. Luckily, Gida is also a master of Karate. As the Reaper targeted Gida's bicep, Gida brought his left hand up and caught the punch. Only able to use his left hand to combat the Reaper made this problematic. That was because Gida's right hand was occupied with creating the ultimate attack. As the Reaper took a step forward and delivered an elbow, Gida spun 360° around while pivoting off his left foot. As he did this, he released the Reaper's hand, allowing him to spin completely around the Reaper to where they were now back-to-back. Gida usually doesn't make such athletic moves, but in this situation, he can't afford any damage to his arms.

Once behind the Reaper, Gida delivered an elbow of his own with his left arm to the back of the Reaper. This blow was filled with Gida's energy, making it strong enough to destroy 13% of a planet. That is all of Australia, Oceania, and 11% of Antarctica. The goal of the blow was to pierce right through the Reaper's back, if it didn't though then the blow would launch the Reaper 729 miles away at ½ the speed of sound. Of course, this all depended on if the blow even connected. Subsequently, Gida thrusts his right hand upwards towards the sky, not caring if his elbow connected or not. This action produced a purplish black aura under Gida's feet that traveled 400 feet in all directions. Anything or anyone other than Gida that was in the vicinity was trapped as they notice themselves start to sink into this purplish black aura. Since the Reaper and Gida were back-to-back this should work. If it does, the Reaper will notice his entire lower body sinking into this aura. He will stop sinking once his waist passed through. This purplish black aura is a one-way portal to the Realm of the Dead. The Realm of the Dead is the realm where all spirits go before being judged and sent to either Heaven or Hell. The Reaper's legs were now in this realm unable to come back, leaving just his upper body. With the Reaper trapped, Gida turned around and pointed his right hand at the Reaper while putting his left hand above his head, palm facing the sky. Two balls of energy formed in each of Gida's hands. The one above Gida's head swelled to 400 feet wide and tall while the other, in Gida's right hand stayed the size of his hand. This move is dubbed the name, Apocalypse. After forming these two energy balls, Gida fired a purplish black energy beam from his right hand towards the Reaper at ½ the speed of sound. At practically the same time, Gida's purplish black aura with gold lightning bolts accompanying it erupted from his body. He then flew 400 feet up into the sky at the speed of sound while hurling the massive energy ball down towards the Reaper at ½ the speed of sound. If the energy beam missed the Reaper or didn't kill it, then the energy ball would. This move, Apocalypse, is strong enough to destroy 68% of a planet. That is all of Australia, Oceania, Europe, Antarctica, South America, North America, and 95% of Africa. To play it safe, Gida flew down to the ground to stay out of range of the energy ball. As soon as he landed, he reverted to his Base Form to conserve power and stamina.

When Gida spun around to get behind Shadow Reaper one and elbow him in the back, Gida froze up and was paralyzed. How was this so? Initially the Shadow Reaper was in Gida's shadow to teleport right in front of him. However, now that Gida is in Shadow Reaper one's shadow, this has become a huge advantage for Shadow Reaper one. Shadow Reaper one had earlier attempted to stretch his shadows like snakes slithering across the ground. This was a Shadow Reaper biological attribute, just like the ability to Shadow Warp and Shadow Step. At a basis this is a stun ability that makes the victim susceptible to the movements of the user. Whatever the user does to move themselves, the victim moves in the same manner as a puppet. With Gida being in the Shadow Reaper's shadow directly, this was where Shadow Reaper one's strength reached its maximum. Gida is unable to physically move as Shadow Reaper one stood still without moving. However, he started to slowly move his arm up and forward from his side to point directly at the space in front of him. Gida did the same except in the opposite direction, and thus would only be pointing at the space in front of him as well.

Shadow Reaper one starts to chuckle as the rest of his shadow and aura form the same tendrils as before and all expand, shooting towards Gida at close range and the speed of sound. All the tendrils were aimed to pierce Gida twenty times all over his body. The tendrils contained the strength and cutting ability to drill through steel with ease. Before this could happen, the Shadow Reaper was alarmed by the dark aura expanding of 400 feet as he was caught within. So was the other Shadow Reaper. Their lower halves are covered and sucked into the Realm of the Dead by this aura. However, they both laugh as they rise out of the aura like it had no effect on them. They were too familiar with the concept of the dead and a land for them.

"You fool! We are Shadow Reapers! The first beings to even possess the ability to meddle with souls and send mortals to where they belong when they are dead!" Shadow Reaper one said while holding out his hand to summon an orb of some random NGA soldier's soul.

The orb then vanishes.

"We existed before the Shinigami. We exist as their ancestors who maintained both order and chaos in mortal realms. We send them to Hell, Heaven, or even Limbo; the Land of the Lost. We can even kill souls so that they cease from existence; not a trace left of where they went. We may cause thy mortal world chaos as we please; an imbalance of souls that exists in the multiverse." Shadow Reaper one said as he starts to realize the black aura was making their shadows disappear and be covered, setting Gida free of his control.

Right before Gida was set free, Shadow Reaper one shot out his tendrils once more at the speed of sound to pierce Gida in twenty different spots on his body.

Shadow Reaper three Shadow Steps ten feet in front of Gida and starts to run towards him with his blade held closely to his chest in an aggressive guard. When close, he slashed at Gida's shoulder and chest diagonally. The Starblade uses its last bit of anti-energy aura around the blade to deliver the slash to Gida.

Gida stopped, was frozen, could not move at all. When his arm moved on its own accord, he knew something was up. He could hear the Reaper's dialogue but could not respond. The fact that they have so much control over souls was sickening. Who gave them the role of God? This infuriated Gida to no end. Power bubbled up inside him even though he could not move. The Reapers would notice that Gida's aura changed from purplish black to gold. Suddenly, he felt a weight lifted and some pressure released. Was he free now? Regardless if he was or not, Gida didn't care...he was pissed.

"How dare you...how dare you think it is child's play to judge souls and send them wherever you want. That's not right at all, you are not God nor will you ever be Him!" Gida shouted at the Reapers as he walked towards the Reaper in front of him.

As he did, Gida felt stabbing pains all over his body from behind him. This was due to the tendrils stabbing him. A small trickle of blood leaves Gida's mouth as he reverted to his base form. Other than that, Gida continued walking towards the Reaper in front of him with determination. Once five feet away, Gida simply turned his body 90° to the right, avoiding the Reaper's slash. The blade narrowly missed his shoulder, most likely cutting some of Gida's shirt and skin though.

"You two are pissing me off. No more games, I could've ended this a while ago. I have been holding back to make sure I didn't blow away the NGA troops on the mountain." Gida said as his wounds healed.

"Now, however; I'm furious. I'm really REALLY mad." Gida continued as he clenched his fists.

"YOU WON'T HARM OR JUDGE ANYONE'S SOULS EVER AGAIN!!!" Gida shouted as he burst into his Universal Form.

Chapter Ten

Gida's eyes, aura, and clothes all obtained their gold light once more. The sheer magnitude of Gida's power slid the Reapers back 50 feet from him. His body radiated heat 5/6 as hot as the sun (8,284°F). Something strange was going on though, Gida's power was pulsing and radiating. How could this be? It is because Gida's transformation occurred out of rage rather than willpower. He didn't willingly go into his Universal Form. He was so mad that his energy level rose to the point of triggering the transformation. However, it didn't stop there, his power continued to rise until Gida's rage started to cool down. Then and only then did his power level off. Gida's Universal Form has been pushed to the limit as he has now found a new level of power for it. It once was very strong but now it is ridiculously strong thanks to the Reapers.

"I'll make you all pay!" Gida shouted once again as his gold aura with gold energy hands flickered and flared up.

Both Shadow Reapers were wearing the same rogue assassin-like attire with hoods that covered their eyes, and masks that covered their lower faces. Behind their armor their eyes were wide in shock and fear. Not only by the manifestation of such sudden power through anger, but also due to the Universal Form generating brighter light and energy on a higher scale of transcendence. This essentially makes it harder if not impossible for the Shadow Phase ability to work. They both had to go all out if they were to even survive.

"Limbo Drive...Ikuzo!" The two Shadow Reapers said as they start to appear semi-shadow.

The center of their body and their bones were physical. However, towards the outside of their body such as their fingers, feet, and shoulders seem to be a bit ghost-like. When reaching their skin, they were fading away into shadows. In a sense it is as if their aura had integrated into their body and soul to enter this new state where they were semi-shadow. Making it not only harder to hit them due to their greater access to greater velocities, but also because the outer areas of their bodies were intangible. Towards the center and critical areas of their bodies, they were still physical/spiritual and were vulnerable to attacks. Using Limbo Drive, they all now moved at the speeds of Shadow Step, at this point being lightning speed, and moving at a constant velocity with little deviating acceleration. Lastly, what makes this mode elite was that the Shadow Reapers seemed to have limitless reserves of energy and do not tire. They may even disappear for a split second at random intervals of time within their limit in this mode. This limit being two minutes before Limbo Drive is deactivated.

Once they enter this mode, they vanish immediately into Shadow Step speeds and circle around the air. Closing in on both, the right and left sides of Gida. Shadow Reaper three gained power for his Starblade again and attempted to stab right into Gida's ribcage, through his heart. Shadow Reaper one pulls out his dagger and encases it with a denser and darker aura of shadow. It looked more like solid flames that were see through rather than an aura. This one aimed at Gida's side hip. The heat from

Gida seemed to have no effect on the Reapers. This is due to how the source of heat is not in direct contact with them and how direct contact has been limited due to the way their Limbo Drive works.

Gida watched as the Shadow Reapers moved towards him at such slow speeds compared to him. In this form, Gida can move at 4/5 the speed of light (536,493,303 mph). So, like before, the Reapers were moving in slow motion in Gida's eyes. Gida set his sights on Shadow Reaper three, deciding to take him out first. Gida glowed gold before dashing towards the Reaper at 4/5 the speed of light, most likely catching the Reaper off guard. Moving at this speed makes it seem like Gida disappeared then reappeared in front of the Reaper. When Gida is three feet away from the Reaper, he glows gold and rapidly throws punches, kicks, elbows, and knees at 4/5 the speed of light towards him. Due to Gida's superior speed, he attacked the Reaper before he had a chance to use his Starblade. The blows targeted the Reaper's head, face, neck, chest, gut, and legs. After delivering the barrage for five seconds, Gida sensed the other Reaper closing in on him. Gida glowed gold and dashed backwards 500 feet at 4/5 the speed of light, essentially vanishing. If the Reaper thrust the dagger towards Gida's side hip, it will completely miss and might even stab his partner. This is what Gida wanted, both Reapers clumped together.

As Gida slid back, he pointed his right hand at both Reapers and fired multiple gold energy blasts from his hand at them. The energy blasts were each the size of Gida's hand. These energy blasts traveled at ½ the speed of sound and were strong enough to make basketball-sized holes in the ground each. Gida shoots these energy blasts for five seconds before glowing gold and dashing above Shadow Reaper three at 4/5 the speed of light. Once above him, Gida reappears and performs a double down-ward hammer fist on the Reaper's head. If this blow didn't kill the Reaper it most likely broke his neck from such power. After dealing with Shadow Reaper three, Gida set his sights on the last Reaper.

Gida glows gold and dashes behind the Reaper at 4/5 the speed of light, essentially vanishing. Once behind him, Gida reappears and side kicks the Reaper in the back with his right leg. The blow intended to send the Reaper flying 2,187 miles at ½ the speed of sound. Gida's gold aura with gold energy hands accompanying it surrounds his body as he flies in front of the Reaper at the speed of sound. Once in front of the approaching Reaper, Gida will knee him in the chin with his right knee causing all his momentum to stop as he gets launched up 2,187 miles into the sky at ½ the speed of sound. Gida then will fly above the Reaper at the speed of sound. Once above him, Gida will do a front flip into an ax kick with his right leg, targeting the Reaper's left trap muscle and collarbone. This blow will launch the Reaper down to the ground at ½ the speed of sound next to Shadow Reaper three.

"Now I'll finish you both." Gida says stoutly as he gathers up energy into his hands, creating a gold hue around his hands.

Gida then fires a gold energy beam at both the Reapers. This beam travels at ½ the speed of sound. After firing the beam at both Reapers, Gida hovers in the sky looking down into the cloud of smoke. His gold aura with gold energy hands disappears as he awaits to see the damage his attacks did on the Reapers. In total, Gida used enough energy to destroy 68% of a planet.

Both Shadow Reapers at this point were unable to coordinate well, simply because of how Gida was beyond their comprehension of speed. Shadow Reaper three did not see it coming and was caught off guard by the vanish and reappearing. He had no time to react to the first punch. Though after the first punch, there was no resisting the chain of other punches, elbows, knees, and kicks. Most of them hitting though some were able to be somewhat blocked and even somewhat ignored, considering their shadow-like state of being semi-invisible. Shadow Reaper three, however; was still holding on tightly to his Starblade. As Shadow Reaper one missed, he knew he did and saw how his comrade had sustained physical damage. He inverted the grip of his dagger and hit his partner using the end of the hilt instead of the blade, thus no friendly fire.

Shadow Reaper three got in front of Shadow Reaper one. Shadow Reaper one released his Shadow Tendrils that went around Shadow Reaper three and at the blasts to intercept them and block their way from reaching both Shadow Reapers. If they got through the tendrils, Shadow Reaper three had his Starblade out to deflect the blasts and negate them using anti-energy. This was a defense followed up by a backup. However, when Gida dashed to Shadow Reaper three from above and sent a hammer fist down at him, Shadow Reaper three reacted to the situation only after Gida was already at the position and at initial motion. He made it barely in time to block. Not even the anti-energy Starblade was strong enough to fully defend the strike. Thus, Shadow Reaper three was sent crashing to the ground and did indeed break his neck and spine; grunting and coughing out black blood. The Starblade dropping out of his hand.

Shadow Reaper one feared Gida at this point. However, this came as an advantage since he now took precautions. Upon seeing Shadow Reaper three being struck from above out of nowhere and with speeds nearing light speed, Shadow Reaper one suspected he was next. He did not need to comprehend or react on time to the speed. He immediately entered a different state of existence prior to Gida motioning to reach behind him and strike with a kick. This mode was Shadow Reaper one's unique ability that he had once used; Shadow Phase. This was when he was completely shadow-like and intangible like before, where physical and spiritual attacks did not work and went through him, unless these were attacks that can specifically interact and damage a shadow. Not even death reaches Shadow Reaper one when in this state of existence, nor would a kick.

Shadow Reaper one stood there watching Gida attempting to damage him. After the kicks Gida would soon realize they were not working and paused to think or do something else. Such as attempting to use a beam attack again. That is when Shadow Reaper one suddenly switches back to normal with his Shadow Drive to now only be semi-physical and use his Shadow Manipulation. From his shadow way below them along the ground, Shadow Reaper one's shadow stretches on its own in attempt to touch and connect with Gida's shadow. If this works, this will cause Gida to be paralyzed physically and spiritually. However, this possession through shadows is not as strong considering Gida's higher state of power. So, this won't last long. Shadow

Reaper one attempts to attack Gida swiftly. If the Shadow Manipulation works, and if not, this will still be attempted. Shadow Tendrils rise out of Shadow Reaper one's back and all shoot out to pierce into Gida. The tendrils all travel at ½ the speed of lightning and are all in such close range of Gida, making them more difficult to react to. Given the speed boost and power boost from Shadow Drive, the tendrils were capable enough to pierce through metals far beyond the strength capacity of steel. Perhaps piercing through everything and anything to take into the building of the interior of a spaceship. Enough to pierce through 5% of the Earth had it been condensed to an inch. That is all of Australia and Oceania combined.

After failing to land his melee attacks on the Shadow Reaper, Gida thought of a plan.

"My attacks go right through him. What can I d-urgh!" Gida grunts as he tries to move but can't.

Gida struggles to move, slowly moving his arms and legs thanks to his overwhelming power now. At the same time, Gida notices the tendrils being launched at him intending to hit him. Having been hit multiple times before by them, Gida refused to get hit again. His power began to swell allowing him to move quicker before finally breaking free of the Shadow Manipulation.

"Enough!" Gida shouts as his gold aura with gold energy hands bursts from his body producing F5 tornado winds (261-318 mph).

Either the sheer power or the winds will blow the tendrils off their course. This caused some to go right by Gida and some to miss him by a lot.

"Try and stop this...if you can." Gida says stoutly.

After realizing his melee attacks won't work, Gida decides to skip past the first part of his ultimate move, Motherly Hands. Gida begins forming two gold energy balls, the size of his hands, in his hands. While Gida is forming these energy balls, two giant gold hands the size of his body launch out of his aura into the air. These gold energy hands also sproduce two golden energy balls. Each energy ball has enough power to destroy 21% of the planet.

So, in total this attack could destroy 84% of the planet if it hit the ground. That is all of Australia, Oceania, Europe, Antarctica, South America, North America, Africa, and 47% of Asia and the Middle East combined. Thankfully the Reaper is in the air, so the planet isn't at risk.

"Take this! Motherly Hands!" Gida shouts as he fires two gold energy beams from his hands at the Reaper.

These beams merge into one massive beam capable of destroying 42% of the planet. That is all of Australia, Oceania, Europe, Antarctica, South America, and 81% of North America combined. This beam travels at ½ the speed of sound. Regardless of what the Reaper does next, the two gold energy hands fire their energy beams at him too. These two beams will merge into one beam that also travels at ½ the speed of sound. In total the Reaper must deal with two beams being launched at it, both strong enough to destroy 42% of a planet.

After firing his beams, Gida will glow gold and fly at 4/5 the speed of light, behind the Reaper. This speed far exceeds the beams', so

Gida has plenty of time to prepare another attack. As he is behind the Reaper, Gida forms a gold energy ball in his right hand and plants it on the Reaper's back. This energy ball is as big as his hand and has enough power to create a basketball-sized hole in the ground. However, that was not the intention. Gida intended for the explosion on the Reaper's back to launch him forward towards the beams at ½ the speed of sound. If this works, then Gida's beams will have a higher chance of hitting the Reaper.

Shadow Reaper one Shadow Steps back to gain a bit of distance. This allows him to have more time to react to whatever was coming next, knowing Gida had the speed advantage in physical movements now. With the two hands forming out of his aura, Shadow Reaper one uses most of his tendrils to merge together into two larger tendrils that match the strength of these energy construct hands. When Gida sends forth the two beams that merged into one, Shadow Reaper one uses his tendrils to redirect the energy hands to get in the way of the beams. Focusing on control rather than power considering the energy hands already had the power advantage, while the Shadow Tendrils had the advantage in numbers and direction. However, the hands too start to shoot beams that start to melt away the tendrils. Apart from that, there was also Gida who moved behind Shadow Reaper one and pushed him forward with an injury to his back. It was over for Shadow Reaper one.

"Tch…darn son of a…!" The Shadow Reaper cursed under his breath.

The beams collided into Shadow Reaper one and he vanished in the large powerful gold explosion. Shadow Reaper three on the ground, who attempts to get up and leave, would also be caught in the explosion and perish.

"That power…chikara! It far exceeds my squadron of Oculatus Shadow Guards." Someone said in a room that was still rather dark; someone who sensed that his men were killed by an individual with great power.

He was sitting down on a throne but stands up and walks forward to reveal that he was a male with long black hair who had a physically fit and athletic build. He was obviously physically young, despite how long the Shadow Reapers have existed throughout time. However, not clear enough through his full appearance, below his feet were the corpses of a whole NGA military squad.

"Well, let us go see who this powerful entity really is. Guards, Eris, we now make our leave from this place, along with this intruder." He says to his remaining comrades who were in the room.

The four of them leave the room towards Gida. Gida is greeted by an exit from the caves he was fighting the Shadow Reapers in. The explosion reveals a pathway that continues back into the halls and into the fort, no longer underground.

Gida, after destroying the Shadow Reapers, sees an exit. He reverts to his Base Form once again. He had no idea who this next foe will be or if they were even worthy of his full power. That, he would test himself by transforming gradually throughout the fight. This right here is Gida's biggest weakness, not going to full power instantly to crush his opponent. Hopefully that doesn't backfire on him here. Gida falls out of the sky before landing on his feet, cracking the ground a bit. He then jogs into the new exit back into the halls of the fort. He could've used his energy to help him run faster but Gida wants to save as much power as possible. He can regenerate wounds but not power. Going through his transformations multiple times is exhausting for Gida. He has already cycled through his transformations twice. The thought of running out of power causes Gida to clench his fists.

"Tch..." Gida spits.

"My Base Form is enough for this jerk." Gida arrogantly says to himself as he runs through the halls towards the power signatures he felt earlier.

Out of the four signatures he felt, one was significantly stronger than the others.

"Must be the leader and his comrades." Gida thought to himself as he continued running.

Although he was outnumbered and this mission was very important, Gida was excited at the possibility of fighting a new ridiculously tough opponent. Just the thought of it brought a smile to his face and caused his heart rate to increase slightly.